BADMINTON
FOR FUN!

By Shane Frederick

Content Adviser: Mary Ann Bowles, Badminton Coach, Certified U.S. National Umpire,
Member of USA Badminton Board of Directors, 2006 Inductee to USA Badminton Walk of Fame, St. Louis, Missouri
Reading Adviser: Susan Kesselring, M.A., Literacy Educator, Rosemount-Apple Valley-Eagan (Minnesota) School District

Compass Point Books ✦ Minneapolis, Minnesota

Compass Point Books
151 Good Counsel Drive
P.O. Box 669
Mankato, MN 56002-0669

Photographs ©: WizData/Shutterstock, front cover (left); Denis Pepin/Shutterstock, front, back cover (racquets); Carsten Medom Madsen/Shutterstock, front, back cover (shuttlecock); Chris Schmidt/iStockphoto, 4–5 (middle), 27; Glyn Kirk/Action Plus/Icon SMI/Newscom, 5 (right); Hulton Archive/Getty Images, 6; Hulton Archive/iStockphoto, 7, 47; Carl De Souza/AFP/Getty Images, 8–9 (middle); Galina Barskaya/Shutterstock, 9; Beaconstox/Alamy, 10; Sergey Rusakov/Shutterstock, 12 (right); Andreas Gradin/Shutterstock, 12 (left); Mary Evans Picture Library, 13, 42 (right); AndreyTTL/Shutterstock, 14 (left); Newscom, 14 (right), 18–19 (middle); Ovidiu Iordachi/Shutterstock, 15; Stuart Miles/Shutterstock, 16; Karon Dubke/Capstone Press, 17 (top, middle); Feng Yu/Shutterstock, 17 (bottom); LouLouPhotos/Shutterstock, 19 (right); Action Plus/Icon SMI/Newscom, 20; Indranil Mukherjee/AFP/Newscom, 21, 29 (right), 43 (bottom); Aflo Foto Agency/Alamy, 22; Photoshot/Xinhua/Newscom, 23; Tengku Bahar/AFP/Getty Images/Newscom; 24; Kazuhiro Nogi/AFP/Getty Images/Newscom; 25; Greenshoots Communications/Alamy, 26; Tengku Bahar/AFP/Newscom, 28–29 (middle); Brian Stewart/AFP/Newscom, 30; Bay Ismoyo/AFP/Newscom, 31; Jewel Samad/AFP/Newscom, 32–33 (middle); Kyodo/Newscom, 33 (right); Alberto Martin/AFP/Getty Images, 34; Bob Thomas/Getty Images, 35; Herbert Gehr/Time Life Pictures/Getty Images, 36; Robert Laberge/Getty Images, 37; Courtesy of USA Badminton, 38 (top), 43 (top); Graham Chadwick/Allsport/Getty Images, 38 (bottom); Ross Kinnaird/Getty Images, 39; Cathrin Mueller/Bongarts/Getty Images, 40; Malte Christians/Bongarts/Getty Images, 41; HIP/Art Resource, NY, 42 (left); B. G. Smith/Shutterstock, 44 (left); Theodore Scott/Shutterstock, 44 (right); Mark Kauffman/Sports Illustrated/Getty Images, 45.

Editor: Brenda Haugen
Page Production: Ashlee Suker
Photo Researcher: Marcie Spence
Art Director: LuAnn Ascheman-Adams
Creative Director: Joe Ewest
Editorial Director: Nick Healy
Managing Editor: Catherine Neitge

Library of Congress Cataloging-in-Publication Data
Frederick, Shane.
  Badminton for fun! / by Shane Frederick.
     p. cm. — (For Fun!: Sports)
  Includes index.
  ISBN 978-0-7565-4025-8 (library binding)
  1. Badminton (Game)—Juvenile literature. I. Title. II. Series.
  GV1007.F68 2009
  796.345—dc22   2008037567

Visit Compass Point Books on the Internet at www.compasspointbooks.com
or e-mail your request to custserv@compasspointbooks.com

Table of Contents

Note: In this book, there are two kinds of vocabulary words. Badminton Words to Know are words specific to badminton. They are defined on page 46. Other Words to Know are helpful words that are not related only to badminton. They are defined on page 47.

Fun and Fast

Badminton is one of the most popular sports in the world. People of all ages and abilities can play it. They play in their backyards, learn it in their school gyms, and compete on courts designed for the sport. Badminton can be a fun, relaxing game played with family and friends. It also can be an intense, competitive game played at high levels.

Speedy Sport

Badminton is the world's fastest racket sport. The best players in the world can smash shots that reach speeds of more than 150 miles (241 kilometers) per hour.

Ancient Game

Although the official rules of badminton are only about 130 years old, the game's origins can be traced back more than 2,000 years. Similar games were played in ancient Greece and China. The games grew in popularity in India and Europe. By the 1800s, the game turned into badminton. The sport got its unique name when the duke of Beaufort (right) introduced it at his country estate, called Badminton House, in Gloucestershire, England, in the 1870s.

Name Game

Before getting the name badminton, the game was called *poona* in India, battledore and shuttlecock in parts of Asia and Europe, and *ti jian zi* in China.

On the Run

Badminton players must be in good shape to compete at a high level. Even though the court is small and the games are short, badminton players can move a total distance of more than 4 miles (6.4 km) in a single match. That's twice as far as the best tennis players travel in one match, even though their court is much bigger. Badminton tests your conditioning, endurance, and reflexes. Players run, jump, lunge, and make sudden changes in direction to keep the shuttle—the object hit back and forth in the game of badminton—from hitting the ground.

Stay Fit

To be in good condition for any sport, a person should eat a healthy, balanced diet and get regular exercise.

Where to Play

A badminton court looks like a small version of a tennis court. An official badminton court is 44 feet (13.4 meters) long and 17 feet (5.2 m) wide. A doubles court is 3 feet (91 centimeters) wider than a singles court. The top of the net is 5 feet (1.5 m) high.

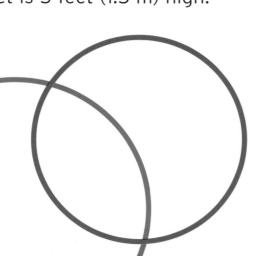

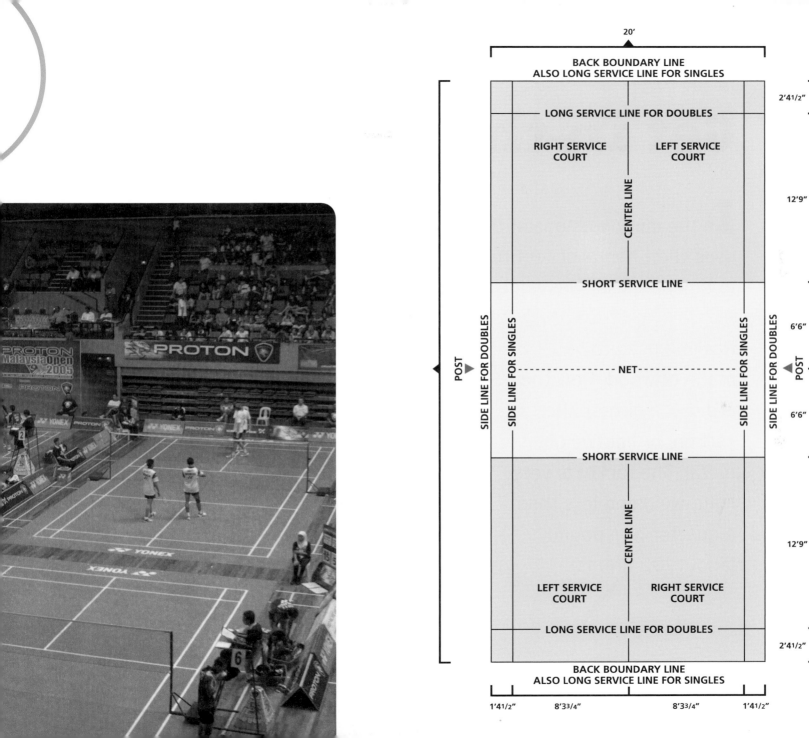

20'

BACK BOUNDARY LINE
ALSO LONG SERVICE LINE FOR SINGLES

LONG SERVICE LINE FOR DOUBLES

2'4 1/2"

RIGHT SERVICE COURT

LEFT SERVICE COURT

CENTER LINE

12'9"

SHORT SERVICE LINE

SIDE LINE FOR DOUBLES

SIDE LINE FOR SINGLES

SIDE LINE FOR SINGLES

SIDE LINE FOR DOUBLES

POST

POST

NET

6'6"

6'6"

SHORT SERVICE LINE

LEFT SERVICE COURT

RIGHT SERVICE COURT

CENTER LINE

12'9"

LONG SERVICE LINE FOR DOUBLES

2'4 1/2"

BACK BOUNDARY LINE
ALSO LONG SERVICE LINE FOR SINGLES

1'4 1/2"   8'3 3/4"   8'3 3/4"   1'4 1/2"

Get in the Game

In the early versions of the sport, players used their hands or feet to hit the shuttle. In time, a racket was added to the game.

Rackets used to be made of wood. Now they are made of graphite, carbon, or lightweight metal. The racket is very light, weighing less than a quarter of a pound (about 100 grams).

Metal racket

Wood rackets

Long Rally

In the game of battledore and shuttlecock, the racket was called a battledore. This game involved hitting the shuttle back and forth as many times as possible before the shuttle hit the ground. In 1830, the record for the number of consecutive hits in a game of battledore and shuttlecock was set at 2,117.

Watch the Birdie

In most racket sports, players hit a ball back and forth. Badminton is a little different. In this speedy sport, players hit a shuttle. The shuttle is unique because it floats slowly when it's hit softly but flies faster than anything else in sports when it's smashed.

Some shuttles look like small birds (above). These shuttles each have a cork base covered with leather, with 16 feathers sticking out of it.

Sometimes the feathers are made of plastic (left) or nylon. Top-level players use shuttles made with goose feathers.

Light as a Feather

The shuttle is also called a shuttlecock, bird, or birdie. It weighs about 0.18 ounce (5 grams). The feathers of a shuttlecock are usually white, but they can be dyed other colors, too.

What to Wear

Since badminton requires so much movement, it's important that players wear the right kind of clothes. The right gear also can help prevent injuries.

Clothing: Badminton players wear lightweight shorts and shirts that give them freedom to move when they run and swing their rackets.

Shoes: Comfortable, lightweight shoes—such as the kind worn for volleyball or tennis—are important. These shoes are flexible but also have strong grips to keep players balanced on the court.

Eye protection: Some players wear glasses or goggles to protect their eyes from flying shuttles.

Headband and wristbands: Badminton is a fast-paced game, and you will sweat. A headband and wristbands will soak up sweat, keeping it out of your eyes and off your racket handle.

Gym bag: You'll need a gym bag to carry your gear. Make sure it's big enough to carry at least two rackets along with your other gear.

How to Play

Badminton is played by two or four players who hit a shuttle back and forth over a net. The object of the game is to win rallies by sending the shuttle to the floor in bounds on your opponent's side of the net. Rallies also end when a player hits the shuttle out-of-bounds or into the net, or if the shuttle touches the player's body or clothing. The winner of a rally gets a point. The first player or team to get 21 points wins the game. Players win a match when they are the first to win two games.

Overtime

A game must be won by two points. So if the score is 20-20, the players keep playing until someone has a two-point advantage, such as 23-21. If the score is 29-29, however, the first player or team to score 30 is the winner.

Swing Low

Every rally begins with a serve (below). Athletes begin play for the point by standing diagonally across from each other in their service courts. The server delivers from the right service court when

Keep It Up

In badminton, the shuttle must always stay in the air. It cannot bounce like the balls can in tennis or racquetball. Once the shuttle touches the floor, the rally ends.

the server's score is an even number and from the left court when the server's score is an odd number. The serve must be delivered to the opponent's service court.

Players must use an underhand stroke for a serve. The server cannot hit the shuttle until it falls below his or her waist and below the hand holding the racket.

Swing Away!

During a rally, players can hit many kinds of shots to try to win the point or get the serve back. Here are some of them:

Drive: A hard, sidearm shot that travels just over the top of the net.

Smash: A fast, powerful overhead shot used to attack and win a rally. A smash is also called a kill.

Smash

Backhand: Any shot hit on the opposite side of the body from the racket hand.

Drop shot: A slow shot, usually overhand, that drops just over the net.

Clear: A shot hit high in the air and deep into an opponent's court. A clear is also called a lob.

Backhand

Winning the Rally

Once you know the different shots, you can use them to try to win a serve, a point, a game, or a match. When you hit the shuttle, you want to use different shots and speeds to send the bird away from your opponent and get him or her moving all around the court. In time, that should create an opening for a smash or another fast shot that will end the rally or force a tough return.

Which Way Did It Go?

Many players use deception when they play. They trick their opponent into thinking they're going to hit one kind of shot or in one direction, but fool them by hitting it differently.

Fair and Square

Fair play and good sportsmanship are important in every sport. In badminton, players have to be honest and accurate. In close plays, players call shuttles in or out-of-bounds. Any shuttle that lands on a line is considered in bounds or good. Players also call faults on themselves—even if it means losing a rally.

A shot close to the out-of-bounds line

Play Nice

Players can practice good sportsmanship by shaking hands before and after a match. They can compliment each other by saying, "Good shot."

Players should call faults on themselves if they reach over the net to touch the shuttle, hit the net with their racket, touch the shuttle with their body or clothing, or hit the bird more than once before sending it over the net.

Singles or Doubles?

Badminton can be played
between two people (singles) or
between two teams made up of
two people each (doubles). In
singles, players have to cover a
lot of ground to keep the rally
going. In doubles, teammates work
together, often with one player
in the backcourt and one player
at midcourt. A doubles court is
3 feet (91 cm) wider than a singles
court. However, the doubles service
courts are shorter. In doubles, like
singles, servers continue to serve
the shuttle until their side loses a
rally. The serve then passes to the

other team. When the serve comes back, the first server's teammate gets to serve.

In mixed doubles, each side has one male and one female playing together as a team.

Need for Speed

How quick is the world's fastest racket sport? The fastest badminton smash ever recorded flew 206 mph (332 kph). Fu Haifeng (right), a doubles player from China, hit the shuttle that fast during a match in 2005. That's faster than the top speed of a NASCAR race car in the Daytona 500!

It's a Birdie, It's a Plane

The wings of privately owned spacecraft SpaceShipOne were designed based on the shape and flight of a shuttlecock. The rocket plane was launched in 2004. When it goes from space back to Earth's atmosphere, the wings fold back, and the machine slows and falls much like a birdie does as it comes down over a net.

In singles competition, Taufik Hidayat (right) of Indonesia hit a shot that went 189 mph (305 kph). To compare, the fastest tennis shot ever recorded was a 153-mph (246-kph) serve by American Andy Roddick.

Where in the World?

Badminton is played all around the world. More than 160 countries are members of the Badminton World Federation. The sport is especially popular in Asia. That's also where some of the best players live.

World Game

The Badminton World Federation is headquartered in Kuala Lumpur, Malaysia.

Only three countries—Malaysia, Indonesia, and China—have won the Thomas Cup (above), a men's team competition created in 1948. Only four countries—the United States, Japan, China, and Indonesia—have won the women's Uber Cup, which was created in 1956.

Going for the Gold

Even though badminton has been a popular sport for many years, it hasn't been an Olympic sport for long. It was an Olympic demonstration sport in 1972 and an exhibition sport in 1988. Four years later, badminton players were finally able to go for the gold. Badminton was added as an official Olympic sport in 1992 in Barcelona, Spain. Indonesia—a country that

The World Is Watching

More than 1 billion people watched the badminton competition on TV during the 1992 Olympics (right). At the 2008 Games, host nation China took eight medals, followed by Indonesia and South Korea with three each, and Malaysia with one.

had never won a gold medal before—took gold, silver, and bronze in men's singles; silver in men's doubles; and gold in women's singles. Malaysia won its first Olympic medal that year, a bronze in men's doubles.

Pasadena Flash

One of the greatest badminton players of all time was an American named Dave Freeman (right). He was known as the "Pasadena Flash," because he was born and raised in Pasadena, California. Freeman was undefeated in singles play from 1939 until he retired in 1953. He was the only American to win a world singles championship, winning the All-England tournament in 1949, the

only year he entered the tournament. He also won seven national titles, including six in a row. Freeman excelled in racket sports. He won tournaments in tennis and table tennis. But badminton was his best sport. In 1940, 1941, and 1942, Freeman won national singles, doubles, and mixed-doubles titles.

It's All Relative

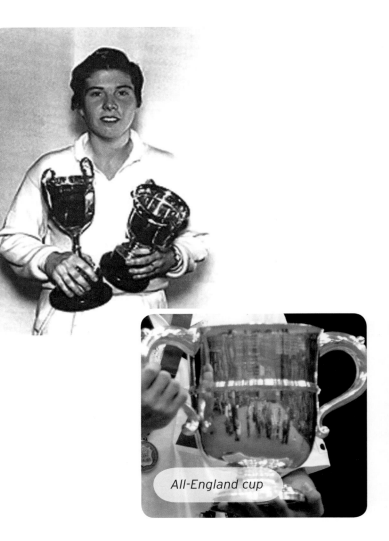

In the 1950s and 1960s, Judy Devlin (right) won more international titles than any other player. She won 12 American singles championships, 12 national doubles titles, and seven mixed-doubles crowns. Devlin won trophies all over the world. Her wins included 17 All-England titles, just one less than her father, Frank Devlin, won in the 1920s. She even won doubles tournaments with her sister, Sue.

All-England cup

Devlin was born in Winnipeg, Manitoba, Canada. As a child, she moved with her family to Baltimore, Maryland. When she was 7 years old, her father started teaching her how to play badminton. Devlin retired from the game when she was 31.

An Evolving Game

Badminton has gone through many changes. Players once kicked the shuttle. Then they used rackets. Later a net was added. People are still making changes to the sport. Recently a new game called speed badminton—or Speedminton— was created. The game uses a heavier shuttle, and players stand in 18-foot x 18-foot (5.5-m x 5.5-m) squares that are 42 feet (12.8 m) apart. There is no net. Players try to hit the shuttle to the opposite

square. If the shuttle lands outside the square, the opponent wins the point. The game is sometimes played on a tennis court.

What Happened When?

5th century B.C.   **1st century** B.C.   **1860**   **1870**   **1880**

5th century B.C. A shuttlecock game called *ti jian zi* is played in China. Players use their feet instead of rackets.

1st century B.C. Battledore and shuttlecock is played in parts of Asia and later would become popular in Europe.

1867 In India, rules are written for the game of *poona*, which includes the use of a net.

1877 The first written rules of badminton are created.

1878 The New York Badminton Club is founded. It is the world's oldest badminton organization.

1873 Badminton is introduced by the duke of Beaufort at the Badminton House in Gloucestershire, England.

| 1930 | 1940 | 1950 | 1960 | 1970 | 1980 | 1990 | 2000 | 2010 |

1934 The International Badminton Federation is created.

1972 Badminton is played as a demonstration sport at the Olympics in Munich, Germany.

2003 USA Badminton opens its Walk of Fame Plaza to honor the sport's best athletes, coaches, and officials at the Orange County Badminton Club in Orange, California.

1956 The Uber Cup competition is held for the first time.

1992 Badminton becomes a full medal sport at the Olympics in Barcelona, Spain.

1948 The first Thomas Cup competition is held.

1996 Mixed doubles are added at the Atlanta Olympics.

2008 China hosts the Olympics and boasts some of the top female badminton players in the world. China earns gold and silver medals in women's singles and gold and bronze medals in women's doubles.

Fun Badminton Facts

The best badminton shuttle feathers come from the left wings of geese. The left wing is considered stronger and has a different curve than the right wing.

The first badminton courts were in the shape of an hourglass.

China and Indonesia have won more than 70 percent of international badminton competitions.

In 1955, Joe Alston became the first and only badminton player to appear on the cover of *Sports Illustrated*.

More than 500 high schools in the United States have varsity badminton teams.

Badminton competitions in Malaysia sometimes draw as many as 15,000 spectators.

The first Olympic gold medalists in badminton, Alan Budikusuma and Susi Susanti of Indonesia, eventually married each other.

Badminton Words to Know

backcourt: back one-third of one side of a court

backhand: shot hit on the opposite side of the body from the racket hand

clear: shot that is hit high in the air and deep into the opponent's court; also called a lob

drive: hard sidearm shot that travels just over the top of the net

drop shot: slow shot, usually overhand, that drops just over the net

fault: violation of the rules that gives your opponent a rally win

game: section of a match; a game ends when the first player reaches 21 points

match: badminton competition; the first player to win two of three games wins a match

midcourt: middle one-third of one side of the court, halfway between the net and the baseline, or back boundary line

overhand: shot delivered over the head that sends the shuttle down to the floor

rally: back-and-forth exchange of shots between two players or teams

return: shot during a rally that sends the shuttle back over the net

serve: first shot of a rally that puts the shuttle into play

service court: area of the court where the serve must be delivered

shuttle: object hit back and forth in a game of badminton; also called a shuttlecock, bird, or birdie

smash: hard, overhead shot that sends the shuttle down toward the floor; also called a kill

underhand: shot delivered below the waist that lifts the shuttle up into the air

GLOSSARY
Other Words to Know

accurate: correct or true

conditioning: exercise to keep a person fit and healthy

consecutive: following one after the other

deception: fooling someone by doing something unexpected

diagonal: line joining two opposite corners of a square

endurance: ability to last through something without wearing down

etiquette: code of polite behavior

graphite: lightweight but strong material often used to make rackets

origins: places where something begins

reflexes: instant reactions to other actions

retired: stopped playing competitively

strategy: plan or method of doing something

Where to Learn More

MORE BOOKS TO READ

Bloss, Margaret Varner, and R. Stanton Hales. *Badminton*. Boston: McGraw-Hill Humanities, 2001.

Paup, Donald C., and Bo Fernhall. *Skills, Drills & Strategies for Badminton*. Scottsdale, Ariz.: Holcomb Hathaway, 2000.

ON THE ROAD

USA Badminton Walk of Fame Plaza
Orange County Badminton Club
1432 N. Main St.
Orange, CA 92867
714/235-6882

USA Badminton
One Olympic Plaza
Colorado Springs, CO 80909
719/866-4808

ON THE WEB

For more information on this topic, use FactHound.

1. Go to *www.facthound.com*
2. Choose your grade level.
3. Begin your search.

This book's ID number is 9780756540258

FactHound will find the best sites for you.

INDEX

ABOUT THE AUTHOR

Shane Frederick is a newspaper sportswriter who lives in Mankato, Minnesota, with his wife, Sara, and three children, Ben, Jack, and Lucy. He covers college hockey and recreational sports for *The Free Press*. He enjoys music, drawing, tennis, and curling.

31901046326221